Northminster E.C.C.
7444 Buckley Road
North Syracuse, NY 13214

Topic: Family   **Subtopic:** Stepparents

Notes to Parents and Teachers:

As a child becomes more familiar reading books, it is important for him/her to rely on and use reading strategies more independently to help figure out words they do not know.

REMEMBER: PRAISE IS A GREAT MOTIVATOR!

Here are some praise points for beginning readers:

• I saw you get your mouth ready to say the first letter of that word.
• I like the way you used the picture to help you figure out that word.
• I noticed that you saw some sight words you knew how to read!

Book Ends for the Reader!

Here are some reminders before reading the text:

• Point to each word you read to make it match what you say.

• Use the picture for help.

• Look at and say the first letter sound of the word.

• Look for sight words that you know how to read in the story.

• Think about the story to see what word might make sense.

Words to Know Before You Read

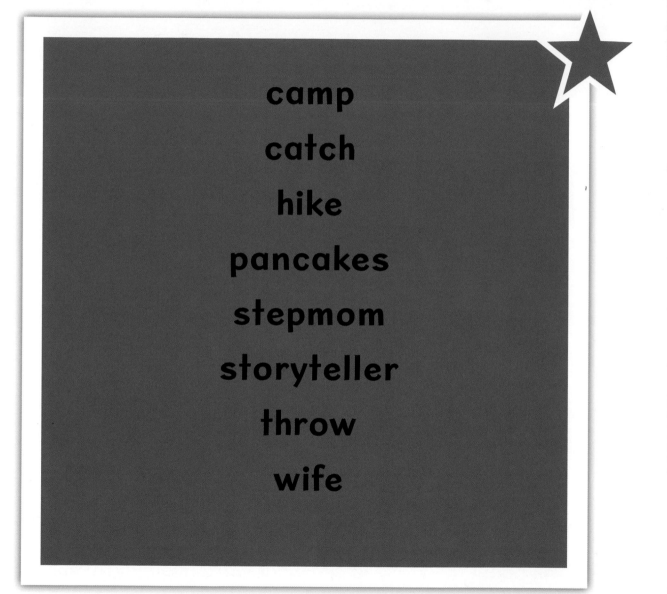

camp

catch

hike

pancakes

stepmom

storyteller

throw

wife

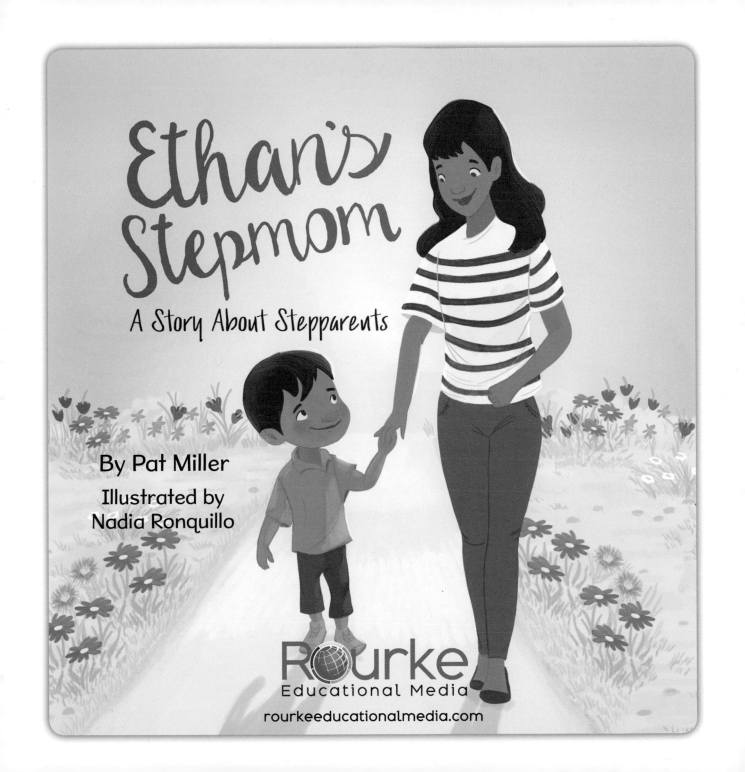

Ethan's Stepmom

A Story About Stepparents

By Pat Miller

Illustrated by
Nadia Ronquillo

Rourke
Educational Media
rourkeeducationalmedia.com

My dad has a new wife.

She is my stepmom.

My mom can throw.

She can catch.

My stepmom cannot.

But she makes me laugh.

9

My mom likes to hike.

She likes to camp.

My stepmom does not.

But she is a good storyteller.

My mom is not a great cook.

But my stepmom is!

She makes pancakes. They look like bears.

She knows when I'm sad.

She knows I miss Mom.

She is not my mom.

But she takes care of me.

Book Ends for the Reader

I know...

1. Name two things Ethan's mom likes to do.

2. Name two things Ethan's stepmom is good at doing.

3. What does Ethan's stepmom do when he is sad?

I think ...

1. Do you know someone with a stepmom or stepdad?

2. What is special about stepparents?

3. How can parents help their children get used to having a stepmom or stepdad?

![Books](books icon) # Book Ends for the Reader

What happened in this book?

Look at each picture and talk about what happened in the story.

About the Author

Pat Miller is an author who lives in Texas. Her mother is a good cook.

About the Illustrator

Nadia Ronquillo was born and raised in Guayaquil, Ecuador. Ever since she could remember, she had a pencil in her hand. She spent her entire childhood drawing and painting in coloring books or sketchbooks.

Library of Congress PCN Data

Ethan's Stepmom (A Story About Stepparents) / Pat Miller
(Changes and Challenges In My Life)
ISBN 978-1-64156-496-0 (hard cover)(alk. paper)
ISBN 978-1-64156-622-3 (soft cover)
ISBN 978-1-64156-733-6 (e-Book)
Library of Congress Control Number: 2018930713

Rourke Educational Media   NOV 0 6 2018
Printed in the United States of America,
North Mankato, Minnesota

Edited by: Keli Sipperley
Layout by: Corey Mills
Cover and interior Illustrations by: Nadia Ronquillo